家人做哪十件事會讓我感覺到愛

文／孟瑛如

圖／許丹又

英文翻譯／吳侑達

阿肥是「一條」快樂的狗，稱呼為「一條」而不是「一隻」的原因，是因為他趴著的時候很扁，像條巧克力。他搖尾巴的速度極快，每次拍打到地板時，總是「啪噠、啪噠」作響！

家人最喜歡看他吃東西時葷素不忌、生熟不忌、好壞不忌，並且速度保證：三秒解決！處理任何食物比垃圾處理器還要迅速確實。但他們卻又常說阿肥太胖了，那些聽起來像是唱花腔的玩笑話，是一連串絢爛高音、層層疊疊、自以為幽默的笑話，但阿肥聽了總是有點難過……

家人總說他是名字取壞了，因為叫阿肥，所以才會那麼肥
……

說他是變種的橘花貓，因為俗話說：「十隻橘貓，九隻肥，
還有一隻特別肥」……

說他是在沙灘上唯一能享受陽光的狗，因為別人都只能在他肥胖身體的陰影下活動……

說他在客廳裡看電視，要先花個 10 分鐘才能將他四處散亂的肥肚皮攤好，所以節目時間還沒到，他就要先坐在電視機前整理肥肚皮……

還說經過他的身邊時會缺氧，因為
他的鼻孔太大，會將空氣都吸走……

家人們也常說些阿肥覺得怪怪的，卻不知該如何是好的話……

媽媽會說：「你都那麼大了，要自己去做……」

奶奶卻說：「你還那麼小，不要自己做，奶奶幫你……」

媽媽會說：「你太胖了，不要吃那麼多！」

奶奶卻說：「餓了趕快吃，不吃飽怎麼行？」

好多矛盾的話，是矛要刺盾？還是盾要擋矛？阿肥都糊塗了！

阿肥也覺得每當別的大人遇到他時，總是要問身高、問體重、問功課，問他這、問他那，讓他覺得自己是個麻煩製造者！

「所以，大家愛我嗎？」阿肥開始有點懷疑。

但當他問媽媽時，媽媽卻很肯定的回答：

「大家當然愛你，他們就是因為愛你，才會問你啊！你有看過他們去問路人嗎？」

「如果愛我，為什麼不能好好愛我，用我喜歡的方式愛我？」

「大人為什麼會問一些不對的或者讓我很受傷的事呢？」

「媽媽都說那是愛我，但我怎麼感覺不到？」

阿肥腦中充滿著大大小小的問號！

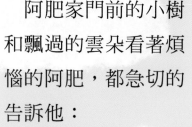

阿肥家門前的小樹
和飄過的雲朵看著煩
惱的阿肥，都急切的
告訴他：

「你要自己告訴爸爸媽媽如何愛你
啊！」

「家就是講愛的地方，說啊！」

「誰最愛自己？就是你自己啊！自
己不說，別人怎麼明白！」

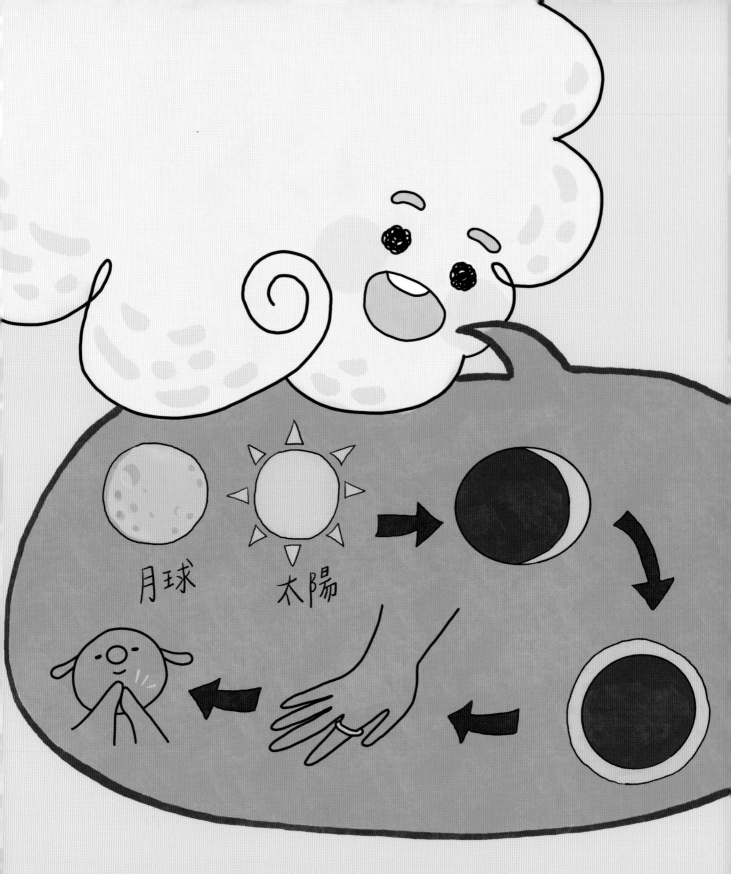

月球　　太陽

　　最大朵的胖胖雲說：「明天就會有難得的日環食現象，這是月球中心與太陽中心最接近的時刻，太陽幾乎會被月球遮擋，僅剩一個亮圈。大家都說那是上帝的金戒指，你可以對著上帝的金戒指禱告，這樣一定會實現願望的！」

　　阿肥決心向上帝的金戒指禱告，因為他想到自己從來沒有告訴過爸爸媽媽怎樣好好愛他！

　　當天晚上，阿肥一直想著該如何告訴上帝，家人做哪些事會讓他感覺到愛。太多了好像很貪心、很自私，太少了又怕說漏了。他想了很久，決定寫下十件事，也就是家人做哪十件事會讓他感覺到愛，因為這就是十全十美！

第一，大家一起愉快的吃晚餐，不要在餐桌上一直問我功課或是我不喜歡的事！

第二，餐桌上放著我愛吃的食物，讓我自己決定吃多少，
不要總是覺得我一定很餓，應該要吃很多！

第三，不要安排我在晚上七點到九點去上才藝課，讓我只能在車上或是路上吃晚餐！

第四，回家開門時給我一個微笑，
就是看到我會很開心的那種微笑！

第五，可以自在的聊天跟分享心事，不要急
著教我，不要急著決定對與錯，單純的跟我分
享今天快樂的事，我也想知道爸爸媽媽的快樂
是什麼！

第六，尊重我的決定，不要覺得我一定不懂事。可以幫我分析利弊，而不是分析對錯，然後真的尊重我，讓我自己做決定！

第七，沒有壓力的陪伴，不要急著想把我「教好」，而只是單純的「在一起」。可以是一起做頓飯、一起看書或看電視、陪我打一場球或玩電動、邊走邊吃冰淇淋、換燈泡、修理家具、幫貓咪洗澡等等。就是只要陪伴，不要壓力！

第八，給我建設性的意見，讓我知道你支持我，而不是拿我跟別人做比較！

第九，跟我說事實，而不
是神話，讓我知道可以感性
想像、理性創造！

第十，記得我的生日，陪我做喜歡的事！

阿肥想得太久、想得太多，竟迷迷糊糊的睡著了！

一覺醒來，才發現早已過了日環食出現的時間！正懊惱不已時，卻發現自己寫得亂七八糟的紙上有著媽媽留下的字：「你就是上天送給爸爸媽媽最耀眼的戒指。趕快來陽台看看每天都有的日環食！」

每天都有的日環食？太不可思議了！阿肥立刻跑到陽台，才發現
家對面頂樓上的水塔與夕陽重疊時的光影，像極了日環食！

爸媽給了阿肥大大的擁抱，

「讓我們一起陪你做喜歡的事！爸爸媽媽真的都好愛好愛你！」

「我也好愛好愛爸爸媽媽！」阿肥露出幸福的微笑！

愛一直都在！

　　「家人做哪些事會讓我感覺到愛？」或許很少有人想過這個問題。絕大部分的人都相信家人間的愛與聯繫，但同時我們也常看或聽到，許多生活在一起的家人不知如何正向講話或表達自己對孩子的愛。常見的溝通迷思例如：(1)愛用反諷口氣跟孩子溝通。就像有時孩子覺得自己穿了這件衣服變得好漂亮，父母明明也這麼覺得，但卻會脫口而出：「哪有？」、「不害臊！」；(2)常在應該提出建議、讓孩子有思考空間學會自我決策時，採強制的「這是為你好」萬用句。「這是為你好」這句話中潛藏著很大的陷阱，無形中未能呈現尊重，換句話說就是「你做的決定比較不好，最好在我設定的範圍內去做決定」或是「依照我的決定去做」，反而是剝奪孩子的自我決策能力；(3)自以為是的幽默卻在無形中傷了孩子。如同故事中的阿肥，家人一方面喜歡看他吃東西，常弄東西給他吃，卻又自以為幽默的用各種方式嘲笑他肥，讓阿肥喪失自信，不知如何是好；(4)比較或是壓力式的對話也容易讓孩子獲取愛的方式失焦。台灣有許多孩子是在「比較」中長大的，你考第三名，父母會問你一、二名是誰，如果考第一名，就會要你繼續維持；你常在及格邊緣浮沉，卻可能有疼愛你的阿嬤說如果你考 100 分，就會給你一百元。懸掛一個幾乎不可能得到的獎勵，以至於孩子也就不在意這個獎勵了。

　　我們可能很愛孩子，但卻很少貼近孩子的生活或個人特質來思考。其實不只要「愛」，還要「懂」；孩子需要沒有壓力的陪伴，尊重孩子是一個獨立的個體，讓他享有屬於自己的成就感，這些都是在相處時需要思考的重點。所以跟孩子溝通很重要，要讓他們能表達或做出決定希望別人怎麼對待自己，故而我讓繪本主角阿肥說出希望家人如何跟他相處的十件事，並說出為何他想這樣做的理由，希望父母或教師都能在「懂」的前提下去愛孩子，可以(1)協助孩子做出如何與他人溝通的決定，提升自我決策能力；(2)尊重孩子的決定，讓他學會自我負責；(3)如果孩子很猶豫而希望你幫忙做決定，那麼先貼近孩子的生活、分析理由，再給出選擇讓他做決定，而非只提供選擇逕自讓他做決定，如此很容易形成犯同樣錯誤或是直覺性的衝動選擇。決定不一定要最好，也不一定要分對錯。「不O.K.也沒關係」（It's O.K. to Not Be O.K.）這句話是女子網球明星大坂直美登上《時代》雜誌（*Time*）封面時的標題。2021 年，大坂直美在其個人推特宣布退出法網：「很遺憾我不能參加今年的法網了，我的腿部仍然感到疼痛，對我來說兩項大滿貫賽事離得太近了，我沒有足夠的時間去準備。」不O.K.也沒關係，更重要的是對孩子心理健康的意識與重視。這不是說我們要教孩子什麼都不管、沒有競爭心態，而是教會他們可以把

焦點放在自己身上，學會溝通與表達，善待自己的身心狀態，並不一定要去配合全世界的期望。

　　大家都說家不是講道理的地方，家是講愛的地方。大家也都說天下無不是的父母，但愛就是愛，愛就是讓孩子活得自在，用他需要的方式來愛他。所以若不能用適合孩子的方式來愛他、站在孩子的角度去想事情、尊重孩子的成長空間，孩子會知道我們愛他，但卻不會真正快樂！大人看到孩子的不快樂，又覺得自己犧牲很多，就會想不通而更不快樂！於是形成惡性循環。這就好像是一場沒有默契的棒球賽，投手與捕手間沒有花時間好好練習與溝通，也聽不進別人的勸告，眼中看不見彼此，只用自己的方式將球丟出，對方卻無法接或是不想接，在漏接與暴投的過程中，很多人生的遺憾就發生了！所以，陪著孩子一起讀這本繪本，然後我們可以運用這本書跟孩子或學生玩接龍遊戲：「家人做什麼事會讓我感覺到愛……」也可以是照樣造句：「朋友做什麼事會讓我感覺到愛……」、「需要我做決定時，我喜歡……」、「我做什麼事會讓爸媽感覺到愛……」、「我做什麼事會讓老師感覺到愛……」、「我做什麼事會讓阿公阿嬤感覺到愛……」、「我做什麼事會讓同學感覺到愛……」、「我做什麼事會讓地球感覺到愛……」等。讓我們都學會正向表達，有自由的成長空間，有受人尊重的生活，用我們喜歡的方式被愛，才是無價的真快樂！

Ten Things that Make Me Feel Loved

Written by Ying-Ru Meng
Illustrated by Dan-You Xu
Translated by Arik Wu

Fatty is a happy dog! Whenever he lies flat on the ground, he looks like a loaf of bread, and is even referred to as a "dog loaf" sometimes. He also has a fast-wagging tail that constantly hits the ground and makes a loud thump.

The whole family loves watching him gulp down any food that comes his way, whether it be meat or vegetables, raw or cooked, bad or good. Three seconds is all it takes for him to "disappear" the food, which seems even more efficient than a garbage disposal unit. However, they often comment that Fatty seems way too chubby. They, of course, mean no harm, but it still upsets Fatty deeply whenever he hears such comments.

The whole family often says that Fatty's chubbiness may be a result of his poorly chosen name—he looks just like an orange tabby cat.

As the famous saying goes, "If there are ten orange tabby cats, nine of which are going to be overweight, and the last one is going to be extra overweight."

They say Fatty seems to be the only dog that gets to enjoy the sunlight when sunbathing on a beach, because the shadow cast by his ginormous body blocks all others from enjoying the rays of the sun.

They say Fatty tends to spend 10 full minutes untangling his saggy skin before watching his favorite TV show, so he always needs to get down early in case he misses the show.

They say people have a hard time breathing as they pass by Fatty, because his nostrils are so big that they seem to suck out all the air.

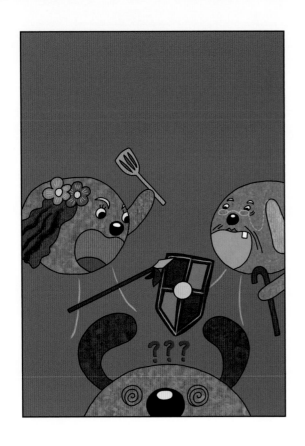

They also give Fatty a lot of confusing orders.

Mom says, "Hey, you're old enough to do this yourself!"

Grandma disagrees by saying, "Well, you're too young to manage this. Let Grandma help!"

Mom also says, "You're way too chubby. Stop eating!"

Grandma again disagrees by saying, "Aren't you hungry? You need to eat more!"

What should he do? Should he listen to Mom, or should he listen to Grandma? Fatty is so confused!

Other adults often ask Fatty about his height, his weight, his schoolwork — everything! He cannot help feeling he is a troublemaker.

"Do they really care about me?" Fatty grows even suspicious of their intents.

When he brings this question to Mom, Mom says with certainty, "Of course they do. They ask you about things because they care about you! Have you ever seen them asking strangers about these things?"

"If you care about me, why don't you do it the way I want you to?"

"Why don't they ask me nicely or ask me about things that make me happy?"

"Mom says they CARE—why don't I feel the same?"

Fatty has so many questions!

The small tree in front of Fatty's house and the clouds that drift by see the confused looking Fatty and decide to try their best to comfort him.

"You have to tell Mom and Dad how you like them to care about you!"

"Home is where love is. Let them know what you think!"

"No one loves you and cares about you more than you do! You need to tell them about your feelings!"

The chubbiest cloud among them says to Fatty, "We are about to see a solar eclipse tomorrow, one of rarest moments when the moon is closest to the ecliptic plane! The moon will almost fully block the sunlight, making the sun look like a ring. People often refer to it as the 'Ring of God*'. You can pray to the ring and I'm sure God will grant you your wishes!"

*Ring of God (also referred to as Ring of Fire).

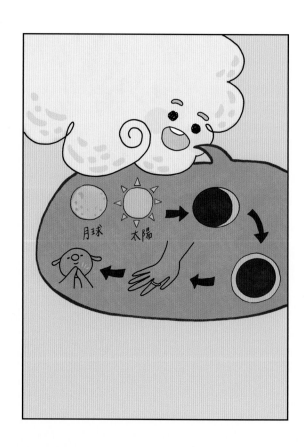

That night, Fatty cannot stop thinking about how he wants his family to love and care about him and how he conveys his wishes to God. Making too many wishes seems greedy, but making too few also seems wasteful. Finally, Fatty decides to write down the ten things that make him feel loved! Ten is such a magical, well-rounded number!

1. Do not ask me about my schoolwork or things I dislike at dinner time. Just enjoy the meal!

2. Serve the food I like and allow me to decide for myself the amount I will eat. Do not assume I am necessarily hungry!

3. Do not schedule after-school lessons between 7 p.m. to 9 p.m., otherwise I will have to finish dinner in the car or on my way there!

4. Smile when I get home. Give me a really, really happy smile.

5. Feel free to chat with me and share with me your thoughts, but do not rush to teach me everything or decide right from wrong for me — just tell me about your day because I also want to know what makes Mom and Dad happy!

6. Respect my decisions. Help me weight the pros and cons, but do not impose your judgment on me. Show respect to me and allow me to make decisions on my own. I may be young, but I am not necessarily naive!

7. Stay with me, without pressuring me or rushing to teach me certain things. Simply being with me is good enough. We can cook a meal together, read a book or watch a TV show, or play a ball game or a video game. Eating ice cream while walking, changing light bulbs, repairing furniture, giving cats a bath are also very nice. Just be with me and do not put pressure on me!

8. Give me constructive suggestions, show me your support and do not compare me with others!

9. Tell me facts, not myths, so that I am allowed to think freely and create rationally!

10. Remember my birthday and celebrate with me by doing what I love !

Fatty keeps on thinking, until he unknowingly falls asleep at one point.

When he wakes up, it is way past the time of solar eclipse, which upsets him greatly. At this moment, Fatty discovers Mom has left a few words on the paper where he put down his ten wishes.

"You're the BRIGHTEST ring God has ever granted us! Come to the balcony and watch the solar eclipse that appears every day!"

The solar eclipse appears every day? How is that even possible? Fatty rushes to the balcony and sees that, when the rooftop water tower across their house overlaps with the setting sun, it looks exactly like a ring.

Mom and Dad come out and hug Fatty warmly.

"Let's do what you love together! Mom and Dad love you so much!"

"I love you too!" Fatty smiles happily.

Love never ends! Love is always there!